# Mickey Mouse
# and the Pet Shop

### ◆ Book Twelve ◆

DISNEP PRESS
New York

Printed in China

First Edition
3 5 7 9 10 8 6 4 2

Library of Congress Catalog Card Number on file

ISBN 978-1-4231-2259-3

For more Disney Press fun,
visit www.disneybooks.com

Mickey Mouse loved animals. So when his friend, Mr. Palmer, had to go on an overnight trip, Mickey was more than happy to watch his pet shop while he was gone.

"I'll be back tomorrow afternoon," said Mr. Palmer as he waved good-bye. "You shouldn't have any problems."

"Have a good time!" called Mickey. "This will be a snap!"

Mickey decided to get to know the animals. They all seemed happy—except for one cute little puppy who wouldn't stop whimpering.

"Poor little fella," said Mickey as he lifted him from his kennel. "What you need is some attention."

But no sooner was the puppy out than he wriggled free from Mickey's arms and raced to the fishbowl for a drink of water.

"Watch out!" screeched the parrot.

But he was too late.

The puppy knocked over the bowl, and the fish went flying across the store.

"Gotcha!" Mickey called as he caught the fish and put it in a new fishbowl. Then he put the puppy back in the kennel.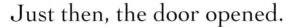

Just then, the door opened. It was Mickey's first customer! He was so excited that he forgot to lock the kennel door.

"Can I help you?" Mickey asked.

Before the customer could even answer, the puppy jumped out of the kennel and set a cageful of mice free. Instantly, the mice began to scurry about the store.

"I'll come back later—much later!" exclaimed the customer as she raced for the door.

After the customer left, Mickey hurried
to gather up all the pets and put them back
where they belonged. And this time, when he
put away the puppy, he made sure to lock the
kennel door.

"Don't worry, little guy," he said to the
puppy kindly. "Someone will take you home
with them soon. You'll see."

By then, it was closing time. So Mickey said good night to all the animals in the shop. Then he turned out the lights and went upstairs to Mr. Palmer's apartment.

Mickey put on his pajamas and climbed into bed. Before he could fall asleep, a loud, howling sound drifted up from the pet shop below.

What was *that*? Mickey wondered. Then suddenly, he knew. It was the puppy!

Mickey scooted down in the bed and pulled the covers over his head. But he could still hear the puppy howling. He covered his ears with his pillow. But he could *still* hear the howls from below.

Mickey gritted his teeth. He couldn't sleep with all that racket. What was he going to do?

Finally, Mickey got up and gave the
puppy what he wanted: a cozy spot under
the covers, right next to him!

When Mickey woke up the next morning, though, the puppy was gone. Maybe he's down in the pet shop, thought Mickey. So he went downstairs to check.

Mickey couldn't believe his eyes when he walked into the store. It was a mess! Books were scattered across the floor, and the plants had all been knocked over. But Mickey still couldn't find the puppy.

Quickly, Mickey got dressed and began to search for the puppy. He looked in every closet and in every cabinet. He looked in every cage and behind every curtain and door. Where could he be? Mickey wondered.

He was just about to give up his search when he suddenly remembered the basement.

Mickey hurried downstairs, to the place where Mr. Palmer stored all his pet food and supplies. And sure enough, to Mickey's relief, that's just where he found the puppy.

Mickey picked him up and carried him back up to the kennel. "Now you can't cause any more trouble," he warned the puppy as he locked the door.

"Now," said Mickey with a sigh, "I suppose it's time to tidy up this store." But as soon as he started sweeping, the puppy began to whimper.

Poor puppy, thought Mickey. He sounded so sad. Mickey felt bad, so he opened the kennel door.

"Now, you have to be good," Mickey told the puppy. And to his surprise, he was!

The puppy helped Mickey finish sweeping and put away all the books. He even helped him dust the countertops.

"You may be a rascal," Mickey told him fondly, "but it sure is nice to have you around."

Mickey and the puppy had just finished cleaning up when Mr. Palmer walked in, grinning.

"It looks like everything went smoothly," he said to Mickey. "I hope none of the animals gave you any trouble."

"It was as easy as pie," Mickey replied.

Then Mr. Palmer handed Mickey his paycheck. "Thanks for your help," he said. "I hope you'll come back soon."

Mickey just smiled, but as soon as he started to leave, the puppy began to howl again.

"I'm going to miss you, too, little fella," Mickey told the puppy. Then a thought occurred to him. What if he took the puppy instead of the paycheck?

The idea was fine with Mr. Palmer. But then Mickey wondered about something else: what should he call the puppy?

Just then, Mickey saw some pictures of outer space on the front of a newspaper. The headline read: NEW PICTURES OF PLUTO!

"That's it!" exclaimed Mickey. "I'll call you Pluto!"